Kitty's Magic

Bobby the Show-Off Cat

Kitty's magic

Bobby the Show-Off Cat

Ella Moonheart

illustrated by Dave Williams

BLOOMSBURY
CHILDREN'S BOOKS
NEW YORK LONDON OXFORD NEW DELHI SYDNEY

BLOOMSBURY CHILDREN'S BOOKS
Bloomsbury Publishing Inc., part of Bloomsbury Publishing Plc
1385 Broadway, New York, NY 10018

BLOOMSBURY, BLOOMSBURY CHILDREN'S BOOKS, and the Diana logo
are trademarks of Bloomsbury Publishing Plc

First published in the United States of America in September 2020
by Bloomsbury Children's Books
www.bloomsbury.com

Text copyright © 2020 by Working Partners Ltd
Illustrations copyright © 2020 by Dave Williams

Bloomsbury books may be purchased for business or promotional use. For information on bulk
purchases please contact Macmillan Corporate and Premium Sales Department at
specialmarkets@macmillan.com

Library of Congress Cataloging-in-Publication Data
Names: Moonheart, Ella, author.
Title: Bobby the show-off cat / by Ella Moonheart.
Description: New York : Bloomsbury, 2020. | Series: Kitty's magic ; 8 |
Summary: When Kitty Kimura magically transforms into a cat, she
decides to help a boastful feline who is trying to hide his homelessness.
Identifiers: LCCN 2020022001 (print) | LCCN 2020022002 (e-book)
ISBN 978-1-5476-0494-4 (paperback) • ISBN 978-1-5476-0495-1 (hardcover)
ISBN 978-1-5476-0496-8 (v. 8 ; e-book)
Subjects: CYAC: Cats—Fiction. | Magic—Fiction. |
Shapeshifting—Fiction. | Japanese Americans—Fiction.
Classification: LCC PZ7.1.M653 Bo 2018 (print) | LCC PZ7.1.M653 (e-book) | DDC [Fic]—dc23
LC record available at https://lccn.loc.gov/2020022001
LC ebook record available at https://lccn.loc.gov/2020022002

Printed and bound in the U.S.A. by Berryville Graphics Inc., Berryville, Virginia
2 4 6 8 10 9 7 5 3 1 (paperback)
2 4 6 8 10 9 7 5 3 1 (hardcover)

To find out more about our authors and books visit www.bloomsbury.com
and sign up for our newsletters.

For Arlo

Special thanks to Natalie Doherty

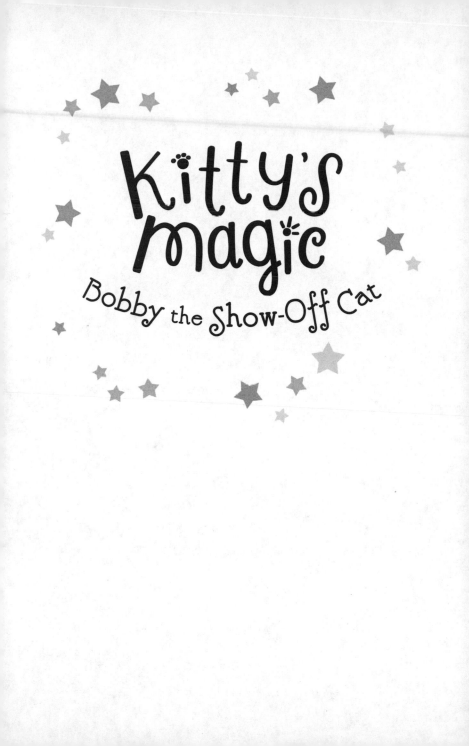

Kitty's magic
Bobby the Show-Off Cat

Chapter 1

Kitty Kimura stared at the clock, watching the hands tick around. Tick, tick, tick. *Move faster, clock!* Kitty thought impatiently.

Next to her, Kitty's friend Mia fidgeted in her seat. In fact, as Kitty glanced around the classroom, she saw that everyone was having trouble staying still.

At the front of the room, Kitty's teacher, Ms. Babbitt, put down the book she was reading to them. "I think we'll finish this chapter another day," she said, smiling. "I can tell everyone is too excited to pay attention. Don't worry, class. Just a few minutes to go!"

As the clock struck twelve, there was a crackle over the loudspeaker. Then Principal Ridge's voice echoed around the classroom. "I am pleased to announce that Fall Field Day has officially begun! Students, please make your way out to the school field!"

Kitty's class cheered and whooped. "Hooray!" cried Mia, bouncing in her chair. "Come on, Kitty, let's go!"

Ms. Babbitt led her students outside

to join the other classes of chattering children. Kitty felt a hand grab hers, and turned to see her friends Jenny and Evie. "Hey, we were hoping we'd find you two!" said Jenny, grinning. "This is going to be so much fun! What games do you think we'll get to play?"

"Maybe tug-of-war?" suggested Mia. "Or sack racing!"

"Ooh, I hope there's the water balloon toss!" said Evie. "That's my favorite."

"Mine too!" agreed Kitty.

"But when the balloons pop, you get all wet!" pointed out Jenny, wrinkling her nose.

"Yep!" said Kitty, laughing. "I love that part best! I don't mind getting wet. Actually, I love it!"

But only in my human form, she thought to herself, reaching up to stroke the pretty silver necklace around her neck. Because Kitty had a very special secret: she could turn into a cat! All she had to do was speak the magic words written on her pendant, and she would transform. The only other person in the whole world who knew this was Kitty's grandma, who lived with her and her parents. She had the same amazing gift! Sometimes Kitty wished she could tell Jenny, Evie, and Mia, because just like her, they all loved cats. She knew they'd love her incredible secret too. But Grandma had explained to Kitty that if she ever told anyone, the magic would be broken forever.

Everything was so much fun in her cat form: racing up tree trunks, chasing after butterflies, and exploring her town in the middle of the night on all four paws. But what she *didn't* like was how it felt when she got wet! If she got caught in the rain, or splashed as a car drove through a deep puddle, it always made her shiver and yowl.

So it was lucky that today she was in human form, because as she reached the school field with her friends, she saw a stack of colorful water balloons, ready for the water balloon toss. "Yesssss!" cried Evie, nudging Kitty.

Before Kitty could reply, she felt someone thump into her arm. "*Oooof!*" she said. Rubbing her arm and frowning, she turned to see a boy pushing through the crowd. "Hey, that hurt!" she called, but the boy didn't seem to hear her.

"Are you okay, Kitty?" asked Mia. "That was pretty rude!"

"That's Brandon," explained Evie, as Jenny sighed. "He's in our class. He can be kind of annoying sometimes."

But Kitty forgot all about Brandon as soon as she saw the rest of the games lined up for Fall Field Day. The whole field was covered in hula hoops, bean bags and balls for juggling, a long thick rope for the tug-of-war, and a huge rainbow parachute. "Let's try that first!" she said, pointing at the parachute, and all four girls ran over to it.

Ms. Babbitt showed them how to spread out around the parachute, along with a few other kids from Kitty's class, and pick up the edge of the silky material. "We're going to play a game called Popcorn," she explained. "I'll throw these foam balls into the middle of the parachute. You have to keep bouncing them high up in the air, and stop them from falling off! Ready, set . . ."

Just as the game was about to begin, someone shoved in between Kitty and Mia, grabbing the parachute. It was Brandon! "I've played this game hundreds of times. I'm the best at it, wait and see!" Brandon announced loudly.

" . . . go!" cried Ms. Babbitt.

She flung a handful of balls onto the parachute. They immediately started rolling toward the edges.

"Quick!" shouted Kitty, and together, she and her friends lifted the parachute up, sending the balls high into the air.

"Great work!" said Ms. Babbitt, clapping.

"They're coming back down!" warned Evie. "Ready?"

"Watch this!" yelled Brandon.

Before Kitty could do anything, he jerked the parachute high into the air. It was snatched out of Kitty's hands.

"Brandon, I can't reach it now!" she said, jumping up to try to grab it back.

On the far side of the parachute, Kitty heard groaning. "All the balls are rolling off!" a girl called. "The parachute isn't flat!"

"*Brandon*," muttered Evie in frustration.

Ms. Babbitt asked a girl from Kitty's class to toss the balls back onto the parachute, and the game started again. "Look how high I can bounce them!" boasted Brandon, flinging the parachute up.

"There they go again," sighed Mia as the balls flew off the parachute and onto the grass.

Ms. Babbitt, frowning slightly, clapped

her hands. "Time to rotate to a new game, everyone," she said.

"Come on, let's head over to the water balloon toss," said Mia.

"Hopefully Brandon won't ruin *that*," sighed Jenny.

Kitty and her friends ran over to the water balloon toss and lined up to play. The teacher in charge, Mr. Rolland, split them into pairs. Jenny and Evie played together, Kitty and Mia next to them. The girls had to throw a water balloon to their partner, taking a step back each time. If you dropped your water balloon, or it burst when you caught it, you were out!

It was easy to start with, but as they stepped farther away from each other,

Kitty found that catching the slippery water balloon became very tricky!

"Come on, Kitty, we can do it!" yelled Mia, flinging the balloon at her.

"Arghh!" cried Kitty, laughing as the balloon hit her in the chest and popped, splashing her with water.

"Yay, we won, we won!" shouted Jenny and Evie, jumping up and down.

"I think you secretly wanted that to happen," giggled Mia, as Kitty squeezed water out of her hair.

Kitty grinned. "Maybe," she replied. "Told you I love getting wet!"

At the end of the day, Grandma was waiting at the school gates to walk Kitty and her friends home. Kitty jumped up to give her a hug. "What a happy Kitty-cat!" commented Grandma, chuckling. "Did you have fun at Fall Field Day?"

"So much fun!" replied Kitty. "We did sack racing, tug-of-war, the egg-and-spoon race . . ."

"Jenny and I won the water balloon toss!" said Evie. "And Mia was brilliant at hula hooping!"

"I wish we didn't have to wait till

spring for the next one," said Kitty sadly. "I wish we could have Field Day every week."

"You have been busy!" said Grandma. "I'm tired just hearing about everything you've been up to, so you must all be exhausted. I think we might both need an early night tonight."

"Hi, Mom!" shouted a voice nearby. Kitty turned to see Brandon racing past her toward a woman with red hair like his. She barely managed to get out of the way in time.

"My, my, he certainly has a lot of energy," said Grandma.

"You have no idea," said Kitty, exchanging a knowing look with her friends.

As Brandon and his mother walked

down the street, Kitty spotted something. Scratched into a telephone pole, right at the bottom, was a small triangle. She nudged Grandma and nodded at the symbol. Grandma's eyes grew wide.

"Someone needs the Cat Council," she whispered to Kitty.

The Cat Council was a secret meeting of all the cats in town, which took place in the woods. Any cat could call a meeting if they needed help with a problem. All they had to do was scratch the special symbol into a tree or a fence post. Kitty had a very important job at the Cat Council: she was the Guardian, which meant she used all her human knowledge to try to help cats who were in trouble.

But who was in trouble this time? As soon as it got dark, Kitty and Grandma would set off for the meeting and find out.

"It looks like we won't be getting an early night after all, Grandma!" whispered Kitty.

Chapter 2

When Kitty's parents got home from work that evening, they wanted to hear all about Fall Field Day. Kitty told them about the parachute game and the water balloon toss, but the whole time, her mind was really on something else. Which cat had called the Cat Council meeting? She couldn't wait to find out, and she hoped she'd be able to help!

"I think it's bedtime, Kitty," said Mom eventually.

Kitty gave her parents a hug and winked at Grandma before she went upstairs. "See you soon!" Grandma whispered.

Kitty brushed her teeth and climbed into bed, but she didn't go to sleep. Instead she watched the sky turn deep inky blue as the moon rose. She heard cats meowing on the street below and knew they were spreading the message about tonight's meeting to any cat who hadn't seen the symbol yet.

Finally, Mom and Dad went to bed too. The moment Kitty heard their door click shut, she threw back the covers and tiptoed downstairs. She had done this so many times now that she knew exactly where the creaky floorboards in her house were and could step right over them. Not even Mom and Dad could know her secret!

When Kitty stepped into the kitchen, a small black cat with a patch of white by her ear was sitting by the back door, which had been left open. Kitty knew

this cat very well: this was Grandma, in her cat form! "You've transformed already, Grandma!" whispered Kitty. "I'd better hurry up!"

She closed her eyes and softly whispered the words on her necklace.

"Human hands to kitten paws,
  Human fingers, kitten claws."

Her nose and ears suddenly filled with a fizzing, whizzing feeling, as if she had gulped down a glass of sparkly cherry soda. The tingling shot through her whole body, spreading into her fingertips and toes. When it faded away, Kitty was nose-to-nose and whisker-to-whisker with the black cat. *She* was a cat, too!

"Let's go!" Kitty meowed and pushed

at the back door with her paw. She sprang out into the yard, feeling the cool, springy grass against her paws and hearing a rustle as Grandma followed. Together they jumped onto the fence, swishing their tails through a line of dandelions, which burst into a swirl of white. Insects chirped and hummed, and frogs croaked in the pond in the yard next door. Kitty was always amazed at how many tiny things she could see, smell, and hear when she was a cat—things she would never notice as a girl.

Kitty and Grandma ran along the fence, darted through yards and alleyways, and squeezed under gates. As she pounced along, Kitty could hear the jingling of the silver collar around

her neck. When Kitty transformed, even her necklace changed!

When Kitty and Grandma reached the clearing, the other cats had already arrived. They sat in a circle, talking in little groups. "Hello, Kitty!" they called. "Hello, Suki!" Suki was Grandma's name.

Kitty meowed hello to them all, and one cat ran forward to meet her: Misty, her best cat friend, who was also Jenny's cat. Kitty and Misty rubbed their foreheads together gently, in a special cat greeting.

"Do you know what's going on?" Kitty asked her friend.

"I'm not sure," replied Misty, looking worried. "But I think there's been some kind of disagreement."

"What about?" asked Kitty.

Before Misty could explain, a big furry tomcat named Tiger spoke up. Tiger was the leader of the Cat Council, and it was his job to start the meeting.

"I think we're all here! Let's begin

with the Meow Vow, please," Tiger announced.

All the cats around the circle chanted the special words together.

"*We promise now,*
This solemn vow,
To help somehow,
When you meow."

When the vow was finished, Suki looked around the circle. "Who called this meeting?" she asked.

To Kitty's surprise, it was Tiger himself who stepped forward.

"I did!" he declared. "I need the Council's help in making an important decision."

Kitty was very curious. She listened carefully as Tiger went on.

"This morning," said Tiger, "I was out for my daily prowl around the neighborhood when I found . . . this."

He pointed a paw at a box of cat treats, which Kitty saw had been placed in the middle of the circle. Kitty knew that to cats, these treats were really delicious. She'd tried them herself once or twice, and her mouth began to water as she remembered their yummy, salty taste. Around the circle, she saw plenty of other cat ears prick up with interest.

"A lucky find!" meowed Suki. "So what is the problem, Tiger?"

A second cat spoke. It was Coco, a very elegant gray cat. "The problem is that Tiger found the box of treats on the sidewalk right outside my house,"

she explained. "I think that means they belong to me."

"But my owner always buys these treats for me!" added a third cat, named Emerald. "She knows how much I love them. They're my favorite! My owner walks along Coco's street on the way home from the store, too. I think she must have dropped the box by accident!"

Tiger looked anxiously at Kitty. "See, Kitty? We don't know how to work out who the treats belong to. Me, Coco, or Emerald!"

"We don't want to argue," added Coco. "But we need to decide what's fair."

"Right," agreed Emerald, nodding.

The cats waited quietly as Kitty

thought. *This is tough!* she said to herself. She didn't want to take sides, because whichever cat she chose, she was sure the others would be upset. And besides, each cat had a good case! It was funny to think that all this had been going on in the cat world today, while she had been busy at Fall Field Day . . .

That's it! thought Kitty. *That's how we can settle this!*

"I have an idea!" she meowed. "We'll have a Field Day, just like the one I had at my school. A *Feline* Field Day! We'll pair up in teams of two, and we'll have lots of competitions."

"What's a competition?" asked one of the kitten twins, whose name was Frost.

"Ooh, I know! It's like a game you have to try and win!" said Misty, swishing her tail in excitement.

Kitty nodded. "The pair who wins the most competitions will get the treats. But everyone else will still get to have lots of fun!"

The Cat Council was buzzing with chatter now. "What kind of competitions, Kitty?" called a cat named Shadow.

"How about tree climbing?" suggested Kitty. "We can have a competition to see who can climb the highest tree. And we could have a jumping competition, too, and a meowing competition . . ."

"Maybe a balancing competition?" added Coco.

"Yes! And lots of races!" meowed Emerald.

"Those are great ideas," Kitty said. "We had races at my school Field Day too! But I know one thing we won't do. The water balloon toss!"

Around the circle, the cats all shuddered. "No, thank you!" meowed Tiger.

"Wait a minute," said Shadow. "What happens if we can't decide who has won a competition?"

"I can sit out and be the referee," offered Suki, stepping forward. "That means I will choose the winner and who gets the treats!"

It was decided that the cats' Field Day would take place in a week's time.

Kitty purred happily as the cats began pairing up. This was going to be so much fun. And Tiger, Coco, and Emerald already looked much happier!

She felt a little nudge and turned to see Misty. "Will you be my partner?" Misty asked hopefully.

"Of course!" Kitty replied. "We make a good team."

Misty and Kitty agreed to meet the next day and start practicing. "Do you think we could win?" Misty whispered.

"I don't know!" said Kitty. "But it's going to be fun trying!"

Chapter 3

Kitty thought she wouldn't be able to get to sleep that night because she was too excited, but she was so tired from Fall Field Day, she fell asleep the minute her head touched the pillow.

The next day, she transformed into her cat form as soon as her mom and dad had left for work at their shop, which sold special Japanese things. She ran down the street and hid in the bushes outside Jenny's house. She knew that on Saturday mornings, Jenny went to soccer practice. Sure enough, before long, her friend came outside with her mom, and they drove away.

The coast is clear! Kitty thought.

Once the car was out of sight, she padded around the back of Jenny's house and into the yard. Misty was waiting and gave an eager meow when she saw her friend.

"What shall we practice first?" asked Kitty, once she and Misty had rubbed heads to say hello.

"How about tree-climbing?" suggested Misty.

"Okay. Race you to the top of that

tree!" said Kitty, and they both leaped at the nearest trunk. Kitty tried to grab it with her kitten claws and pull herself up, but she didn't manage to get very far. The bark was smooth and slippery from last night's rain. Before long, Kitty and Misty both slid back down, landing on their bottoms with a yowl and a thud!

"Hey!" cried Kitty. "I thought we cats were always supposed to land on our feet!"

"At least we know we could win one competition at Field Day. Not tree climbing, but tree *sliding*!" joked Misty.

"That's not the right way to climb a tree, you know," said an unfamiliar voice from behind them.

Kitty and Misty whirled around. A big gray cat was perched on the yard fence, watching them.

"Who are you?" asked Kitty.

"My name is Bobby," the gray cat said, sitting up importantly. "I was walking past when I heard you talking about climbing that tree, and I heard the bump when you fell down! It's easy if you know how to do it. Watch me."

Bobby jumped down into the yard and marched over to the tree. "I can even do it with just my forepaws," he boasted.

Kitty and Misty glanced at one another. "Climbing a tree without using your back paws? That's impossible!" Misty whispered.

They watched as Bobby leaped at the trunk, scrabbling to grip it just like they had done. "I thought you weren't going to use your back paws," Kitty said doubtfully, as the gray cat dug all four sets of claws into the bark.

"Oh, I was, um, only kidding about that!" said Bobby quickly. "Hey, look,

I'm doing it! Told you, didn't I? I'm the best at climbing trees!"

Bobby managed to get only a little way up the trunk before tumbling back to the ground. "See, I said it was easy!" he said, jumping back up.

"Easy? I think he was even worse than us," muttered Misty.

Bobby pretended not to hear her. "I can't wait to win all the competitions at Feline Field Day. And the treats!" he announced.

"How do you know about Field Day?" asked Kitty. "You weren't at the Cat Council meeting last night."

"I overheard some cats on my street talking about it," Bobby told her. "I just need to find a partner, but I'm not worried about that. Everyone will want to pair up with me! Hey, want to see how fast I can race?"

Before waiting for an answer, he charged across the yard, almost running headfirst into Jenny's trampoline.

"What a show-off!" said Misty. "Come on, Kitty, let's practice our jumping. If we dip our paws in the mud and jump at the wall, we can make pawmarks and measure how high we get!"

But Bobby, realizing they weren't watching him anymore, was running back toward them. "Jumping? Oh, I'm the BEST jumper. I bet I can jump twice as high as either of you!"

Misty's fur was bristling, but Kitty didn't want to be unfriendly—even though Bobby was a little annoying! "Okay, why don't we all dip our paws in the mud and see how high we can jump?" she suggested patiently.

But without waiting, Bobby pushed past both kittens and leaped into the muddy patch at the edge of the garden, splashing Kitty and Misty's coats with mud.

"Urgh!'" cried Misty.

"Oops!" said Bobby. "Sorry, but if you were as quick as me, maybe you would have been able to move out of the way in time. Anyway, watch this!" He ran toward the wall and jumped as high as he could, leaving muddy prints on the bricks. "Now it's your turn, but you definitely won't beat me," he called.

Kitty sighed. This was no fun! And she could tell that Misty felt the same. She wished Bobby would go away, but how could she ask him to without seeming mean?

"Oh, I think I hear something," she said, pricking up her ears and turning to Misty. "It sounds like your humans are back already. You'd better go inside, Misty. I should head home too."

"Really?" said Misty, frowning. Then her eyes widened as she realized what Kitty was doing. "Oh, right! Yes, I can hear them!" she said quickly.

Bobby paused, trying to listen. "Oh, I heard them ages ago!" he said, although Kitty knew he couldn't hear anything. "I have *amazing* hearing. Well,

I'd better get back to my family, too. They'll be waiting for me, probably with a big bag of my favorite snacks, and some new toys! I have the best family in the world. We live in the biggest, nicest house in town. You should come and hang out some time!"

"Oh, uh—thanks?" said Kitty, as Bobby scampered off.

"See you at Field Day!" he yelled as he disappeared over the fence.

"Thank goodness he's gone!" meowed Misty when the sound of Bobby padding away had faded. "I can't believe he's going to be at Field Day. He's going to ruin it for everyone! I've never met such a show-off, have you?"

Kitty agreed. "Although, well, it's funny, but he really reminded me of someone!" she said. "But I don't know any cats who behave like that . . ."

Chapter 4

Kitty spent the rest of the weekend puzzling it over. Who did Bobby remind her of? She just couldn't think of any cats who behaved like he did.

On Monday morning, she met Jenny, Mia, and Evie, and they walked to school together, Jenny giggling as she told them how she had slipped in the mud at soccer practice on Saturday and somehow scored a goal by accident. As they approached the school gates, something caught Kitty's eye. Another triangle—this time, carved into a fence post.

Another Cat Council meeting already? she thought. *We just had one a few days ago! I wonder what's wrong now?*

But before she could give it any more thought, she heard Evie groan. "Brandon," Evie muttered. "Just ahead of us. And guess what. He's showing off. Again!"

Kitty looked up. Brandon was perched on the school gates and holding a shiny toy car. "It's new! My mom bought it for me this weekend," he was bragging to any kid who would listen.

"*That's* who Bobby reminded me of!" exclaimed Kitty. It wasn't a cat she'd been trying to think of—it was a human! "Brandon!"

"Who's Bobby?" asked Jenny.

Oops. Kitty hadn't meant to speak out loud! "Uh, just someone I saw on TV this weekend," she said quickly, hoping she wasn't flushing. Luckily, Bobby was a human name as well as a cat name. If she had said Whiskers or Tabby, her slip-up would have been much harder to explain!

Kitty and Suki made their way to the clearing for that evening's Cat Council meeting once Kitty's parents were in bed. But tonight felt very different from the last meeting. Even before they had arrived, Kitty could hear cats complaining. "We have to do something!" Tiger was saying grumpily, as she and Suki joined the circle.

"What's going on?" Kitty whispered to Misty, who was already there.

"It seems like we're not the only cats who Bobby annoyed this weekend!" Misty replied.

"This is about Bobby?" said Kitty, surprised. She looked around the circle and saw that every cat looked upset or angry, and that Bobby was not among them.

"He spoiled our meowing practice," explained Frost, as her sister Snowdrop nodded. "We only have tiny little meows because we're just kittens, so we wanted to get better! We tried meowing as loudly as we could. Then Bobby showed up and told us we'd never be as loud as him. Snowdrop was really sad, and I told Bobby to go away!"

"Bobby jumped into my yard and told me he was amazing at balancing," Coco added darkly. "He tried walking along the washing line, but my owner had just pinned out some white sheets to dry. Bobby got muddy paw prints all over them, and my owner thought it was me. She was very angry and took my favorite mouse toy away!"

"Bobby broke *my* owner's favorite flowerpot," said a little cat named

Scout sadly. "He was bragging that he could catch a butterfly, but he wasn't looking where he was going and he crashed into it. He didn't even say sorry. He just ran off. My owner was so upset!"

"I think we're all agreed that Bobby should not be allowed to come to Feline

Field Day," said Coco, and all the cats meowed in agreement.

Kitty listened quietly, a little knot of worry forming in her tummy. She agreed that Bobby was annoying and that Field Day probably wouldn't be as much fun with him there. But she felt bad for Bobby, too. He had seemed so excited about joining the games. If he was the only cat not allowed to take part, he would feel left out!

Kitty glanced across at Suki and saw that she was looking anxious too.

"Grandma," Kitty whispered, "I think we should let Bobby join in."

Suki nodded. "I think you are right, Kitty," she replied.

"The Cat Council is supposed to help other cats, not be unkind to them," Kitty said, her voice shaking slightly. It wasn't easy to disagree with the rest of Cat Council! "If we leave Bobby out, wouldn't that be unkind?"

Kitty waited nervously as the cats all murmured to one another. Then Tiger spoke up. "You're right, Kitty," he said. "Thank you for reminding us. The Cat Council should never exclude anyone."

"But he won't find a partner," said Coco. "Who would want to pair up with him?"

Kitty paused. "Well, *I* could be Bobby's partner," she said.

"Wait a minute!" said Misty. "Kitty, we're partners!"

"I know! But someone has to pair with Bobby, otherwise he won't be able to join in," explained Kitty, feeling miserable.

"But if you partner with Bobby, that leaves me by myself," said Misty. "Then *I* won't be able to take part!"

"Bobby should get to join in, but it's not fair if Misty can't join in," piped up Frost. "She hasn't done anything wrong."

"I have an idea. Misty, what if I'm your partner?" suggested Suki.

"But you're our referee," pointed out Emerald. "How will we know who the winner is?"

"We'll all be the referees," explained

Suki. "We can take turns judging the different events and decide on the winner together."

"Grandma, that's a great idea. What do you think, Misty?" asked Kitty hopefully.

Misty sighed. "Well . . . okay," she agreed. "But I still don't think it's a very good idea, Kitty. Bobby is going to ruin it for everyone!"

The rest of the Cat Council thought so too. Everyone seemed very unsure about letting Bobby take part.

"I'll talk to him," promised Kitty. "I'm sure Bobby can behave himself!"

But as she and Grandma headed back home that evening, she found herself thinking, *What have I done?*

After school the next day, Kitty asked Grandma if she could go to the park. Mom and Dad would be at the shop for another hour or two, and Kitty had important things to do!

"Be home for dinner!" Grandma said, waving goodbye at the park gates. Kitty didn't waste any time and found a big, shady sycamore tree at the park's edge to duck behind. When she was sure no one was looking her way, she quietly spoke the special words on her necklace.

"*Human hands to kitten paws,*
Human fingers, kitten claws."

Once she had transformed into her cat form, she made her way to the playground. At the end of last night's

Cat Council meeting, she had asked the other cats to tell Bobby to meet her there if they saw him today. As she turned off the path into the playground, she spotted Bobby and realized her plan had worked.

Kitty couldn't help feeling a little sorry for him. Bobby was by himself, she saw. It seemed as though all the other cats in town were keeping their distance. He looked very busy, though, charging around the playground on some kind of obstacle course. First, he ran up the slide. Then he jumped down, leaped through the tire swing, and landed on the monkey bars. Then he trotted along the top, balancing very carefully.

Kitty was surprised. He was actually pretty good!

"Hi, Bobby!" she called.

Bobby turned eagerly. "Oh, hi, Kitty!" he said. "Shadow and Coco told me to meet you here. I'm really excited to be your partner at Field Day!"

"Oh, well, me too!" said Kitty. *This is*

going well, she thought, feeling pleased. *He's not so bad.*

"You're really lucky. Now I can teach you all my skills," continued Bobby. "You'll definitely win now that you're on my team."

Kitty managed not to let out a sigh. Why did Bobby have to ruin everything by bragging so much? No wonder he was here by himself! More than ever, he reminded her of boastful Brandon.

"Well, let's start practicing," she said, doing her best not to show Bobby she was annoyed. "Maybe we could run along the top of the monkey bars, like you were doing just now? That looks like fun."

"I bet you've never seen anyone run along the top of the monkey bars like me," Bobby said proudly, leaping up the metal frame. "Watch!"

Instead of trotting along it carefully, this time Bobby tried to balance on just one front paw and one hind paw at a time. He was very wobbly, and he almost fell through the bars once or

twice. *I have to get him to do it normally,* Kitty thought, *before he hurts himself!*

"Wow, I've never seen anyone balance like that," she said. "But the field day will be all about speed. Don't you think it would be faster to use all four paws?"

"Oh, okay!" Bobby trotted along the top of the bars quickly. "Like this?"

"That's great!" said Kitty, following behind. She had been right. When Bobby wasn't trying to show off, he was much faster.

They moved around the playground, from the monkey bars to the slide to the merry-go-round. Once Kitty had persuaded Bobby not to try jumping from the merry-go-round as it was whizzing around, they both took turns sitting on it, with their tails flying. It was a lot of fun. And, Kitty realized, so was Bobby—that is, when he wasn't trying his hardest to impress anyone!

Soon it was time for Kitty to head home. "I have to go. My dinner will be ready soon," she explained.

Bobby's whiskers drooped, but only for a second. "Oh, mine too," he told her quickly. "In fact, I can hear my owner calling me right now! I live in a big, big house nearby. Well, it's more of a mansion, really. See you, Kitty!"

As Bobby ran off, Kitty frowned. A mansion? She had never seen a mansion in her town before! And she was pretty sure she hadn't heard anyone calling Bobby's name just now, either.

I'm going to find out what's going on, she decided, setting off after the big gray cat.

Kitty stayed back so that Bobby wouldn't hear her collar jingling and crouched in the shadows in case he turned around. All the way through town they ran, until Bobby turned down a quiet street. The house he stopped at wasn't a mansion at all, but a cozy-looking cottage with flowers in the front yard. A bowl of water was waiting on the doorstep.

Bobby gulped the water down. But then, instead of going inside the cottage, he kept running down the street.

That's odd, thought Kitty.

As she followed Bobby, she saw him stop several more times at different houses, drinking bowls of water and nibbling at snacks that people had left outside. Finally, he headed for the last house on the street.

Kitty stared at it. Bobby had been telling the truth . . . sort of. It was a very big house, with a porch and a turret, and it looked like it must have been very grand once. But it also looked very spooky! The windows were broken and covered in cobwebs. The huge yard was wild and overgrown. And there was a big sign nailed to the front fence that said: KEEP OUT. DANGER.

Kitty was sure that no one lived in

this house—and that no one had for a very long time.

But as she watched, Bobby slipped under the crooked fence and through one of the broken windows.

I can't believe it, thought Kitty. *Bobby doesn't live in a big house with a family who loves him. Bobby doesn't have a family at all!*

Chapter 5

Kitty ran home from the old, abandoned house, thinking all the while about poor Bobby. By the time she arrived at her house and transformed back into her human form, her mom and dad were starting to get worried.

"There you are!" said Dad, giving her a big hug. "Kitty, it's almost dark."

"I know! I'm sorry," Kitty said.

"Where were you, Kitty-cat?" asked Mom.

"I . . . I found a cat wandering around at the park," she explained. "A big, gray cat." She glanced at Grandma, and Grandma gave a tiny nod to show she understood that Kitty was describing Bobby. "I followed it home. I was trying to make sure it got back to its family safely."

"Such a kind Kitty-cat," said Grandma, smiling. "And did you?"

Kitty shook her head. "No!" she said, feeling tears prick her eyes. "I don't think this cat *has* a family!"

Grandma's eyes widened. Kitty knew that Grandma would be as upset and worried by this news as she was. They

both knew that cats needed a safe home and a loving family more than anything.

Mom was looking concerned too, but for a different reason. "Kitty, it was very sweet of you to try to help, but I'm not sure you should be getting too close to cats. Remember, you're allergic to them."

"I know, Mom," replied Kitty, nodding. "Don't worry; I didn't pet him."

Her eyes met Grandma's again in a knowing look. For most of her life, Kitty had believed she *was* allergic to cats. Her nose would always itch and twitch when she was around one. But now she knew that those itchy, twitchy feelings were just her magical gift trying to get out! Since she'd found out about her special secret and transformed into a cat for the very first time, her "allergies" had totally disappeared. Of course, she couldn't tell Mom and Dad that.

When Kitty's parents went into the kitchen to finish making dinner, Kitty told Grandma the whole story. "He lives in an abandoned house, Grandma. All the windows are broken, and there's a sign on the door saying DANGER!" whispered Kitty. "It looks like some of the families on his street leave out water and snacks for him, but he doesn't have a family of his own."

Grandma nodded, her face lined with worry. "We have to think of a way to help him, Kitty-cat," she said.

"I know. But Bobby has told every cat

in town about his huge house and his amazing family," said Kitty, sighing. "I don't think he wants anyone to know the truth."

"Then perhaps that's what you should do first," suggested Grandma. "Convince Bobby to tell the truth!"

The next day, Kitty went straight to the abandoned house after school. The street was quiet, so she hid behind a tree and transformed. Once she was a cat, she padded along the sidewalk and slipped under the broken fence.

She found Bobby around the back of the house, practicing for Feline Field Day by balancing on the top of the wonky old fence. Kitty could see that he was very determined. Just like yesterday, when he wasn't showing off, he was really good!

"Hi, Bobby!" she called.

Bobby almost fell off the fence. "Kitty!" he said, startled. "What are you doing here? How did you find me?"

Before Kitty could answer, he quickly added, "Oh, I don't live here, if that's what you're thinking! No, it's just a great place to practice all my skills! Isn't it cool?"

As gently as she could, Kitty said, "Bobby, I followed you here yesterday, from the playground You're here all by yourself, aren't you?"

When Bobby didn't answer, she went on. "It's nothing to be ashamed of," she said. "But if you don't have a family, I might be able to help you."

"Of course I have a family!" yelped Bobby. "Why would a cat as great as me not have a family? I have the best owners in the world, they—"

There was a noisy *crack*. Kitty gasped as the rickety old fence post underneath Bobby gave way! With a yowl, Bobby fell onto the ground in a heap of broken wood.

"Bobby, are you okay?" called Kitty.

Bobby tried to climb free. "Ouch!" he meowed. "Kitty, help! My tail's stuck!"

"Wait there!" said Kitty. She glanced all around, checking there was no one else in sight. Once she was sure they were alone, she muttered the words on

her collar and transformed back into her human form. Even as the sparkling sensation swept through her, and a sound like bubbles fizzing in a drink filled her ears, she could hear Bobby meowing in shock.

Kitty couldn't help giggling at the amazed expression on Bobby's face as the fizzing feeling faded and she opened her eyes again. "I have a special gift," she explained. "I'm really a girl, but I can turn into a cat whenever I want to. So can my grandma! Now, let's take a look at that tail . . ."

Gently, she managed to free Bobby's tail from where it was trapped among the pieces of broken fence. As she touched it, he hissed and arched his back.

"Oh dear," said Kitty, as she looked more closely. "I think you've got some splinters of wood in your tail, Bobby. We need to get you to the vet!"

Carefully, she picked Bobby up and cradled him in her arms, trying not to touch his injured tail. Then, as quickly as she could, she walked him home. Luckily, Mom and Dad were still at work. When Grandma came to the door, she understood at once. "We'll go straight to Dr. Gomez," she said. "She'll be able to help."

Dr. Gomez's veterinary office was only a few streets away. When Grandma and Kitty arrived, with Bobby curled in Kitty's arms, the receptionist took one look at Bobby and said, "It looks like you need an emergency appointment. I'll ask Dr. Gomez if she can see you right away."

Soon, the vet was bandaging up Bobby's tail. Kitty held him while she did, stroking his fur gently. "You're being very brave," she whispered.

Dr. Gomez smiled at her. "He's very lucky to have such a kind owner," she said.

"Oh, he's not mine!" Kitty replied, without thinking.

Dr. Gomez frowned. "Really? Then who does he belong to?"

Kitty glanced quickly at Grandma, who shook her head. "Uh . . . well, actually he's a stray," Kitty admitted.

"Then he's even more lucky to have met you," Dr. Gomez said. "When stray cats get hurt, their injuries can be very nasty because they have no owners to bring them to a vet. I think the best place for Bobby is the cat rescue center, unless we can find a real home for him soon."

Kitty felt Bobby freeze in her arms. The people at the cat rescue center were all very kind, but the cats who lived there weren't allowed to roam freely around the streets or run through the woods at night. All the things cats loved best! And there was no telling how long it might take them to find a family to adopt them.

Why did I say he was a stray? thought Kitty, feeling very mad at herself.

"For now, I'll keep Bobby here with me," said Dr. Gomez, reaching out to take him from Kitty. Carefully, she put him in a kennel with some cozy blankets inside and shut the door. "I'll make sure he has a good meal and a warm place to sleep tonight, and I'll keep an eye on his tail. I'll call the cat rescue center tomorrow."

Kitty didn't want to let Bobby go, but she knew she had to. Mom and Dad would never agree to Bobby coming to live with them, because they thought she had an allergy to cats! It looked like he was staying with Dr. Gomez tonight. Then tomorrow, he'd be taken to the cat rescue center.

Unless . . .

"Don't worry, Bobby," whispered Kitty, bending down and looking inside the kennel as Grandma was thanking Dr. Gomez. "I won't let you go to the cat rescue center. I'll find you a real home, you'll see!"

Chapter 6

Kitty was very quiet on the way home. She couldn't stop thinking about Bobby. What was she going to do? How was she going to find him a home?

As she and Grandma stepped inside, she saw her school bag hanging on a hook by the front door, covered in cat stickers. She, Jenny, Evie, and Mia had all decorated their bags together. *That's it!* she thought suddenly. *My friends will be able to help!*

"Grandma," she said, "may I use the phone?"

"Of course, Kitty-cat," said Grandma.

Quickly, Kitty called her friends. One by one, she told them that she needed to meet them in the park. "It's an emergency," she told them. "A cat emergency! I'll explain properly when we get there. See you by the swings in ten minutes!"

When the girls had all arrived, Kitty told them about Bobby. Jenny, Mia, and Evie all loved cats as much as Kitty did, and gasped when she described the empty old house with its broken, dusty windows. "He doesn't have a family," she finished. "We need to find him one—fast!"

"Poor Bobby!" said Mia. "He sounds lovely, Kitty. I'm sure there must be lots of people who would love to adopt a cat."

"Where should we start?" asked Evie. "We can't knock on every door in town, can we?"

Kitty had an idea. "The houses that left water and food out for Bobby! We'll start there," she said.

"Good plan," said Jenny.

Kitty led them to the street where she had seen Bobby visit several houses and knocked on the first door—the cozy cottage. A friendly-looking man

with glasses answered. "May I help you?" he asked.

"I hope so!" replied Kitty, smiling. "We're looking for a home for a really nice cat. His name is Bobby and he's big, fluffy, and gray."

"Oh, is that the stray who comes into my yard sometimes?" said the man. "I try to feed him when I can. The problem is, I have to go away a lot for work. So, although I love cats, I can't have one myself."

"Oh. Well, thank you anyway," said Kitty, feeling disappointed.

As Mia knocked on the next door, the girls heard a noisy yapping sound. "Dog alert!" whispered Evie.

When an elderly lady opened the

door, Kitty explained that they were looking for a home for a stray cat, but she had already guessed what the answer would be. "I'm very sorry, girls, but as you can probably hear, I have three dogs," said the lady. "Very noisy dogs! So, as much as I'd like to help, I don't think my house is the best place for a cat."

Kitty thanked her, and the lady closed the door. They went from door to door, but none of the families on this street could give Bobby a home. "I'm terribly allergic," explained one lady. "I'm afraid I sneeze every time I'm near one. It's such a shame, because I love cats!"

"I know the feeling," said Kitty, and her friends all smiled sympathetically.

Finally, there was just one house left.

"Fingers crossed!" said Evie as she knocked on the door.

As it swung open, the girls gasped at the familiar face before them.

"Brandon!" said Kitty in surprise. "You live here?"

Brandon stared at them all, eyes wide. "What are *you* doing at my house?" he asked. "Wait . . . I bet you've heard

about my new swing set, right? And you've come over to see it! It's the coolest!"

"Here we go," muttered Evie under her breath.

"Shh!" said Kitty, nudging her. "Uh, no, that's not why we're here, Brandon. We wanted to talk to you about a cat."

"Brandon, who are you talking to?" asked a voice, and Brandon's mom appeared at the door. "Hello, girls," she said, smiling. "Did I hear you say something about a cat? Brandon and I love cats, don't we, Brandon?"

"Really?" said Jenny, looking surprised. "*You* like cats, Brandon?"

"Yes!" said Brandon, grinning. "There's a big gray cat who lives on this street, and he always comes to visit me."

"That's the cat we wanted to talk to you about!" said Kitty. "His name is Bobby, and he doesn't have a family. I found him up at that old abandoned house. He'd hurt his tail, so I took him to the vet. Dr. Gomez is going to take him to the rescue center if we don't find a home for him!"

"Oh, goodness. The poor thing," said Brandon's mom. "We didn't realize he was a stray, did we, Brandon?"

Brandon shook his head. "We thought he must belong to another family around here," he explained. "Mom, can *we* have Bobby?"

Brandon's mom hesitated. "Well, Brandon, having a cat of your own is a really big responsibility," she said.

"I know that! I'd take such good care of him," said Brandon eagerly. "I promise, Mom! Besides, don't you think Bobby would rather come to live with a family he already knows, instead of strangers?"

"I suppose that's true," Brandon's mom said. "I'm just not sure . . ."

"Oh, please, Mom," begged Brandon. "Bobby and I love playing together in the back yard. He's my only real—"

Brandon stopped suddenly, blushing. Kitty had a feeling she knew what he'd been about to say. *He's my only real friend.* Just like Bobby, Brandon always tried hard to impress everyone around him. *Is this why?* Kitty wondered. *Is it because they're both lonely and want to make friends?*

Brandon was looking awkwardly at

the ground, so Kitty stepped in. "I can see why you and Bobby get along so well," she said kindly. "You're both lots of fun. You'd be a great owner for a cat like Bobby."

Brandon blushed an even deeper shade of pink, but he looked up at his mom hopefully. "So, can we adopt Bobby? Pleeeease?"

Brandon's mom smiled. "Oh, okay! Your friend is right. You *would* make a good cat owner, Brandon. And it sounds like Bobby needs lots of love! We'll go straight over to the vet's office now."

"Yessssssss!" Kitty and her friends cried, leaping into the air. "We did it!"

Brandon's mom chuckled. "Perhaps you could join us," she suggested to

Kitty. "Since you're the one who brought him in to Dr. Gomez."

"Yes, please!" said Kitty, smiling. "I'll just say goodbye to my friends, so I'll see you there."

As Brandon and his mom rushed off, chatting excitedly, Kitty and her friends gave each other a big hug. "Yay! Bobby has a family!" said Evie happily.

"A great family. Brandon's mom seems nice, doesn't she?" said Mia.

"And Brandon does too!" added Jenny, sounding surprised. "If he loves cats that much, he can't be as bad as we thought, right?"

"Right," said Kitty, smiling. "It seems like he really cares about Bobby."

Once the girls had said goodbye, Kitty ran toward the vet's office, taking a shortcut through the park—a shortcut she had learned on one of her nightly adventures as a cat! She got there before Brandon and his mom, and burst through the doors.

"Hi, Dr. Gomez!" she said breathlessly. "Guess what? I found a family for Bobby. And they're coming to get him right now!"

"Goodness!" exclaimed Dr. Gomez. "That's wonderful news, Kitty. We'd better go and get Bobby ready."

Kitty followed the vet into the room where Bobby was safely tucked away in the kennel. Dr. Gomez unlocked the door and Kitty gently lifted the cat out, taking care not to touch his bandaged tail. "Hello," Kitty whispered to him. "Bobby, you're going to a real home, and it's a really great one, I promise!"

The door swung open, and Brandon and his mom walked in. Brandon's face lit up when he saw Bobby. "I can't believe he's going to be my cat," he said happily.

"Here, you should hold him," Kitty said, passing Bobby gently to Brandon. She watched as Brandon hugged Bobby and stroked his fur, and smiled as Bobby began to purr loudly.

"Well, you two seem very happy with one another," said Dr. Gomez, looking pleased.

Kitty decided to slip away quietly, so

that the new family could enjoy some time together. She mouthed, "See you soon," to Bobby and tiptoed to the door. As she pushed it open she caught Brandon's eye. He gave her a huge grin and said, "Thanks, Kitty."

"You're welcome," said Kitty, grinning back.

Chapter 7

The next day, the woods were buzzing with the sound of cats purring and meowing, as the Cat Council gathered at the clearing.

This time, though, they weren't there for a meeting. It was time for the Feline Field Day at last!

Cats were sitting in their pairs, whispering and talking excitedly. "I can't wait to try the branch balancing," Coco whispered to her partner, Ruby.

The only cat missing was Bobby.

Tiger stepped into the middle of the circle. "I declare this Feline Field Day open!" he called proudly. "We will begin the first game in just a moment!"

Kitty sat on the grass next to Suki and Misty. She glanced around, looking hopefully beyond the circle of cats. *Where is he?* she thought. *He has to show up soon!*

"Never mind, Kitty," Suki said gently. "Bobby must be really busy settling into his new home. He probably couldn't slip away without his family noticing!"

"His family that *you* found for him,

Kitty!" Misty reminded Kitty, nudging her friend. "You really helped Bobby out."

"I know," said Kitty, nodding. But she couldn't help feeling a little sad. She was really happy that Bobby had found a home, but she wished he had turned up today. Without her partner, she wouldn't be able to join in the games at Field Day. And she had hoped the other cats would get a chance to see Bobby again, behaving nicely this time.

"Cats, please take your places next to the big oak tree," called Tiger. "We're going to start with the long pounce! That means we're all going to do our biggest, longest, springiest pounce."

"Good luck!" said Kitty, trying to sound cheerful as the cats began to step forward. Just then, she heard a meow behind her, and turned around.

"Bobby!" she exclaimed. "You came!"

"Sorry, Kitty. I'm a bit late, aren't I?" said Bobby nervously. He was stepping forward a little slowly, and Kitty saw that his tail was still bandaged up. "I, er, wanted to say sorry for what I did. I didn't mean to lie to you about not having a family or a home. But . . . I just couldn't tell you the truth."

"Oh, that's okay, Bobby," said Kitty gently.

"I did have a family once, you see," Bobby explained. "Then they moved away, and they didn't take me with them. They just left me. I didn't know what to do. I was so lonely! I found that big abandoned house and decided I would live there instead."

Kitty gasped. "I can't believe anyone would do that," she said. "That's awful, Bobby."

Bobby nodded sadly. "I thought it

must've been because I did something wrong," he said. "Or maybe I just wasn't good enough to have a family. So I thought I could at least try to make some cat friends. That way, I wouldn't be by myself anymore! I tried to impress the cats in town so that they would like me."

"Oh, Bobby!" said Kitty, shaking her head. "You didn't do anything wrong. It was your family who wasn't good enough for you. Not if they treated you like that!"

"Do you think so?" said Bobby hopefully.

"Definitely!" said Kitty firmly. "And I know your new family would never do that! Brandon loves you so much already. His mom seems like such a nice lady too."

Bobby immediately started purring. "She's great!" he agreed happily. "This morning she bought me the coziest bed, and a big box full of new toys. She even had a cat flap put into the front door so I can jump in and out whenever I like. But Brandon is the best human ever! We spent the whole day playing together. That's why I was a little late. I was having so much fun, I almost forgot."

"That's okay!" said Kitty. "You're here now, just in time. But . . ."

"What?" asked Bobby, as Kitty hesitated.

"Well, you don't have to try to impress any of the cats here," Kitty told him. "Really! It's much better to just be yourself—and to have fun."

"Okay," said Bobby uncertainly. "I'll try, Kitty."

"Great. Now let's go, quick!" said Kitty, and she bounded over to join the other cats lining up to take part in the long pounce. "Wait for me and my partner!" she called.

"Uh oh. Bobby's here," muttered Coco. All the other cats were looking worried too.

Kitty whispered to them, "Just give him a chance, okay?"

"Ready, cats?" called Tiger. "Set . . ."

The cats all hunkered down low, pressing their bodies flat against the grass. Kitty smiled as she caught sight of Bobby's determined face, his injured tail still curling excitedly.

"Go!" cried Tiger.

With loud, eager meows, the cats all jumped forward as far as they could. "Wow!" purred Misty, looking around excitedly. "I think I won! Did I win?"

Kitty looked along the line. "Yes!"

she said happily. "You jumped the farthest, Misty. And Bobby, you came second."

Don't brag, Bobby! she thought to herself. If she had been in her human form right now, she would have crossed her fingers!

But she had no reason to worry.

"Well done, Misty!" said Bobby. "Great pounce. Maybe you can teach me your technique sometime."

Misty purred proudly, and Kitty saw that lots of the cats were looking in surprise at Bobby. "What's next?" she called.

"Branch balance relay," decided Tiger. "We'll take turns to run halfway along that long, low branch, then tag your partner to run the rest of the way."

Chatting excitedly, the cats bounded up the tree trunk two by two, taking their places for the partner relay. There were meows of friendly laughter as some cats wobbled and fell off the branch, landing lightly on their paws. Kitty wondered if Bobby might try to do something daring, like run along the branch backwards or on just two paws. But when it was their turn, he took a deep breath and ran along it carefully, swinging his bandaged tail in the air to balance. He made it all the way to where Kitty was waiting without a single wobble. He tagged Kitty with one paw and she darted off, running the rest of the way along the branch and then jumping down to the ground when she'd reached the end.

When all the cats had taken their turn, it was Suki who called out, "I think Bobby and Kitty were the best branch-balancers. What does everyone else think?"

"I think so too," agreed Frost, and Snowdrop meowed and nodded.

Bobby looked delighted, but instead of bragging that he had won, he said thank you to everyone. "I couldn't have done it without Kitty," he said.

"You're doing great," she whispered back to him as they got ready for the yowling competition.

"I'm just being myself, like you told me to," whispered back Bobby. "You were right, Kitty. I don't need to work so hard to impress anyone."

After the high-paw jump, the tree-trunk climb, the ball-of-wool dash, and the puddle-dodge challenge, all the cats were panting and very tired, but having a lot of fun. And everyone was ready to find out who the winner of the Feline Field Day was!

"Everyone has done very well," announced Tiger. "And I don't even mind that the prize is going to some-one else. It's been so much fun! Today's winners definitely deserve the snacks, especially as one of them has a hurt tail! The pair that won the most competitions is . . . Kitty and Bobby!"

The cats cheered. "We did it!" cried Kitty, meowing happily.

Bobby was purring so noisily that Kitty thought that all the humans in town might wake up! "I've never won anything before!" he said.

"Well, here. The treats are yours," said Tiger, nudging the box toward Bobby with his nose.

Bobby reached out and tore open the top of the box with a claw. "Mmmmm," he said. "These smell really tasty!"

He looked around at the Cat Council, and then at Kitty. "I wouldn't have been able to join in today if Kitty hadn't been so kind to me," he said.

"And you all gave me a second chance to take part, too! So, to say thank you, I'd really like it if we could all share these treats. If you don't mind, Kitty?" he added quickly. "This is your prize too, after all."

"That's a great idea," replied Kitty, feeling a purr deep in her belly.

"Yum! Thanks, Bobby," meowed Coco, picking up a treat with her teeth.

"My favorite," sighed Emerald happily, crunching into her own treat.

Soon, all the cats were nibbling at the delicious treats. As Kitty enjoyed her own, she settled down on the grass beside Misty, Suki, and her new friend, Bobby. When he was being himself, he

really was a pretty cool cat. Just like Brandon was actually a pretty cool boy. Kitty couldn't wait for school tomorrow, to talk to her new friend about his new cat!

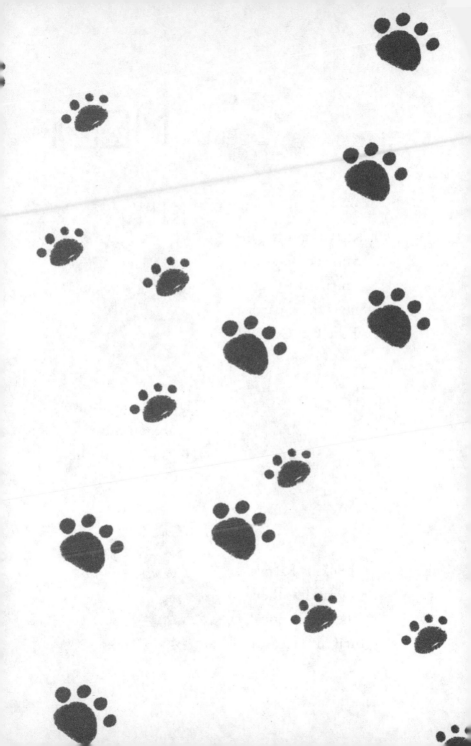

MEET

Kitty

Kitty is a little girl who can magically turn into a cat! She is the Guardian of the Cat Council.

Tiger

Tiger is a big, brave tabby tomcat. He is leader of the Cat Council.

Suki

Suki is Kitty's grandmother. She can magically turn into a cat too!

THE CATS

Misty

Misty is Kitty's best cat friend. She is the cat with the longest pounce.

Emerald

Emerald is a very fancy white cat with green eyes. Emerald has a big heart.

Bobby

Bobby is a big gray cat who loves to run, jump, and play, especially with his new owner, Brandon!

FELINE FACTS

Here are some
fun facts about our
purrrfect animal friends
that you might like
to know . . .

When they aren't sleeping,
cats spend up to half of
their time grooming
themselves.

In one Japanese train
station, the stationmaster is
a calico cat named Nitama.

3.

In some countri[es] black cats are considered lucky.

4.

The average cat can run up to 30 miles per hour.

5.

In the 1870s, a Belgian city tried to train cats to deliver the mail. But it turned out cats didn't make very good mail carriers!

Ella Moonheart grew up telling fun and exciting stories to anyone who would listen. Now that she's an author, she's thrilled to be able to tell stories to many more children with her Kitty's Magic books. Ella loves animals, but cats most of all! She wishes she could turn into one just like Kitty, but she's happy to just play with her pet cat, Nibbles—when she's not writing her books, of course!